First published by Parragon in 2012
Parragon
Queen Street House
4 Queen Street
Bath BA1 1HE, UK
www.parragon.com

Edited by: Katrina Hanford
Designed by: Pete Hampshire
Production by: Emma Fulleylove

ISBN 978-1-4454-6501-2

Printed in China

Playtime Stories

Bath · New York · Singapore · Hong Kong · Cologne · Delhi
Melbourne · Amsterdam · Johannesburg · Auckland · Shenzhen

Contents

The Circus Comes to Town

Written by Melinda LaRose
Illustrated by Alan Batson

Zip! Zoom! Ellyvan and Zooter
race through Jungle Junction.
Suddenly, Ellyvan stops. He sees
a brand-new sign!

What does it mean?
"The circus is coming to town!" says Zooter.

The sign leads to Miss Jolly's school. "We can't wait to see your circus!" says Zooter.

"How would you like to be in my circus?"
asks Miss Jolly.

"Wowie-zowie! I would love to!" says Zooter.
"Me, too! Me, too!" says Ellyvan.

What will Ellyvan and Zooter do
in the circus?

Taxicrab is the circus juggler. "My juggling is as smooth as my smoothies!" says Taxicrab.

The Beetle Bugs are acrobats.
"Ta-da!" cry the Beetle Bugs.

"My two wheels are perfect for the high wire," says Zooter.

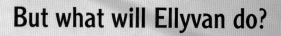

But what will Ellyvan do?

"How about the trapeze?" asks Bungo. "You can soar through the air with the greatest of ease!"

Ellyvan closes his eyes and jumps off the platform!

THUD!

"Am I doing it?" asks Ellyvan.
"Not quite," says Bungo.

"How about the seesaw?" asks Zooter.
"You can tumble and twirl!"

The Beetle Bugs jump on the seesaw.
Uh-oh! Ellyvan doesn't budge.

"Am I doing it?" asks Ellyvan
"Not quite," says Zooter.

"Sorry, Miss Jolly. I guess I'm too big for the circus," Ellyvan says sadly.

Just then, Taxicrab trips and bumps
into the tent pole!

Whoa! The tent is falling!

Ellyvan holds up the tent
with his trunk!
"You saved the day,"
says Miss Jolly.

"And you found a circus act!"
says Zooter.
"I did?" asks Ellyvan.

Miss Jolly starts the circus. "Presenting... the Jungle Junction Circus!"

Zip, zip! The Amazing
Zooter rides the
tightrope on one wheel!

Hup-hup! Taxicrab the
Great can juggle anything!
Even Toadhog!

Whoosh! Bungo the Magnificent flies over the crowd!

**Boing-boing! The Bouncing Beetle Bugs
build a pyramid!**

"And now," announces Miss Jolly, "the strongest strongman in Jungle Junction – Ellyvan!"

"Am I doing it?" Ellyvan asks Zooter.
"You sure are!" says Zooter.

Bravo! The circus stars take their bows!
The Jungle Junction Circus is a big hit!

Toadhog's Trouble

Written by Melinda LaRose

Illustrated by Alan Batson

Ellyvan and Zooter are playing catch.
Suddenly, they hear something....

"Does not!" says Bungo. "Does, too!" says
Toadhog.
Oh, no! Toadhog and Bungo are
fighting!

Toadhog got lost going to the mud pond!
"This sign points to the mud
pond!" says Toadhog.

"It does not," says Bungo. "That sign is for the Coconut Grove."

"Bungo, your signs are silly!" shouts Toadhog.

Bungo takes his sign and rolls away.

"Toadhog!" says Zooter. "That wasn't very nice. You hurt Bungo's feelings."

"Maybe you should say you're sorry," says Ellyvan.

"Harrumph!" says Toadhog.

Oh, no! Bungo is so upset that he
takes down all his signs!

Taxicrab is going to the banana tree.

But without seeing a sign, he doesn't know where to go!

Not that way! **Splash!**

Hippobus is driving the Beetle Bugs to school.

"Hmm, which way do I go?"
she wonders.

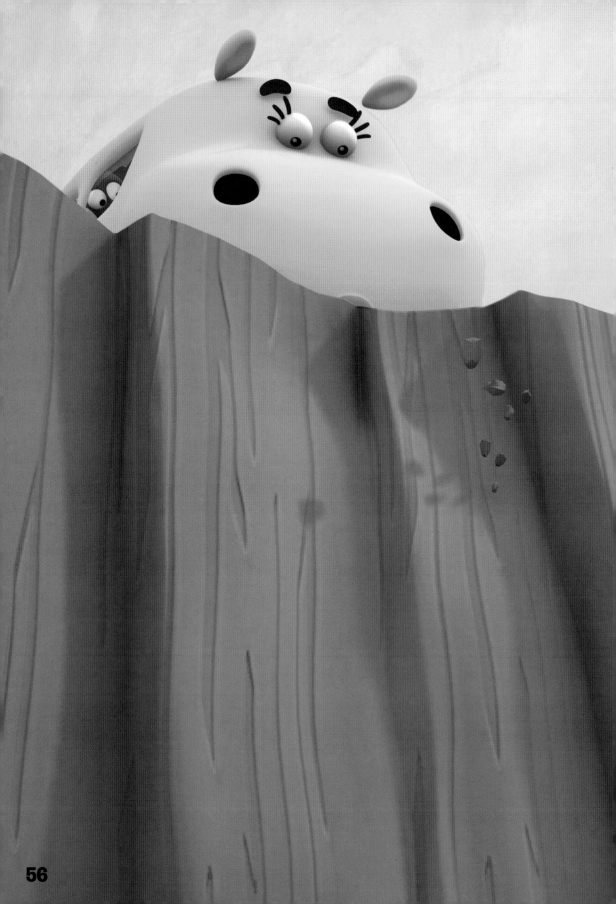

Whoa!
Not that way!

"I don't need Bungo's silly signs,"
says Toadhog. "I can find the
mud pond myself."

Not that way! **Buzzzz!**

"Have you seen Hippobus?" asks Miss Jolly. "The Beetle Bugs are not at school!"

"Which way to the banana tree?" asks Taxicrab. "I can't make smoothies without bananas!"

Suddenly, Toadhog races by.
He's being chased by a swarm
of bees!

"Ahh!" cries Toadhog.

"Oh, dear," says Zooter. "We need Bungo's signs!"
"Toadhog, you have to apologize to Bungo,"
says Ellyvan.

"All right, all right," says Toadhog.

Zooter, Ellyvan and Toadhog go to Bungo's warren.

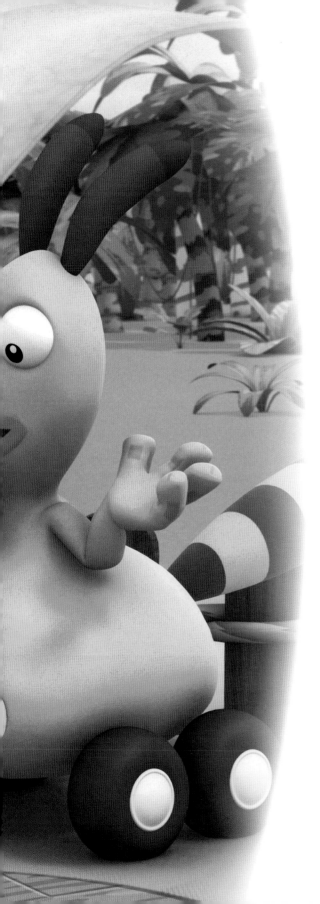

"Bungo, you make the best signs in Jungle Junction," says Toadhog. "And... I got lost without them. I'm sorry."

"Well, okay," Bungo says with a smile.

69

Toadhog helps Bungo put back all the signs.

Hippobus brings the Beetle Bugs to school.

Taxicrab picks loads of bananas!
"Smoothies for everyone!" he says.

And as the sun sets on Jungle Junction, two friends enjoy banana smoothies and a nice mud bath.

Redfinger

By Marcy Kelman
Illustrated by Alan Batson

"Hmmm, my ball landed
somewhere around
here. Where could it be?"
Juan wondered.

"It must be in here," Juan said as he reached into the rosebush and felt around for the football. **"OUCH!"**

Juan forgot that rosebushes have very sharp thorns!
"Oh, no!" Juan cried when he saw the cut on his finger.
"Now what should I do?"

CLICK! Shutter Bug found someone in need of Special Agent Oso's help. Shutter Bug sent out a special alert!

"Special Agent Oso? Mr Dos here. Juan just hurt his finger at the playground and doesn't know what to do! Your special assignment: help Juan bandage his finger."

"Sounds like a plan!" said Oso. "Paw Pilot, what special steps will I need for this assignment?"

"Three special steps, that's all you need!"
replied Paw Pilot.

Can you help Oso put these steps in the right order?

"What is the code name for today's
special assignment, Paw Pilot?" asked Oso.

"Today's code name? It's **Redfinger**! So let's race
to the playground – there's no time to linger!"
said Paw Pilot.

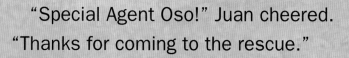

"Special Agent Oso!" Juan cheered.
"Thanks for coming to the rescue."

"Glad to help out, Juan." Oso motioned towards the bathroom. "No time to waste, we've got to take care of that finger, pronto. Follow me!"

"Step one: wash the cut with warm, soapy water," guided Paw Pilot.

"Oh, no, this water is too cold," Oso noted.
Which tap should we turn on to make it warm?

Oso smiled. "Good idea! Turning on the hot water tap made the cold water warm."

"Ahhh, my finger feels better already," Juan smiled.

"Step two: use a towel to dry off your hands,"
said Paw Pilot.

"Then add a dab of antiseptic cream to stop the cut from getting infected," explained Oso.

Oso scratched his chin. "Gee, there's one more step, but I just can't remember what it is."

Do you know what the third and final step is?

Yes, put a bandage on the cut!

"The bandage will keep out dirt and germs and will help Juan's cut heal," explained Paw Pilot.

"Now it's time to tackle this rosebush."
Oso slipped on some heavy-duty work gloves and quickly found Juan's ball hiding in the thorny branches.

"Touchdown!" Juan cheered. "Great play, Coach Oso!"

"Now make sure to wash your finger and change your bandage every day," advised Oso. "Before you know it, that cut will disappear completely!"

Juan beamed. "Thanks, Special Agent Oso!"

"Assignment complete!" called Paw Pilot.

"Will you share my digi medal for all of your help on this mission?" asked Oso. "I couldn't have done it without you!"

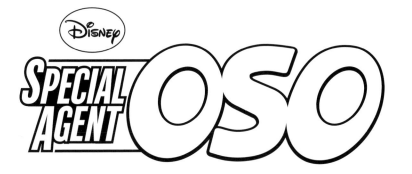

You Always Look Twice

By Marcy Kelman

Illustrated by Alan Batson

"Are you ready for today's training exercise, Oso?"
Dottie asked. Special Agent Oso grinned.
"Dodging paintballs? You bet!"

"Great! Now remember, the paintballs will be coming at you from the left and from the right," explained Dottie, "so be sure to look both ways before crossing the hallway."

"Most importantly, you need to first look right, then left and then right again before moving forward," said Dottie.

"Got it!" Oso laughed.

Oso waited in the hallway.

"Okay, the paintball machines will turn on in ten seconds," Dottie called from the control room.

"Ready, Oso?"

"You know it, Dottie!"

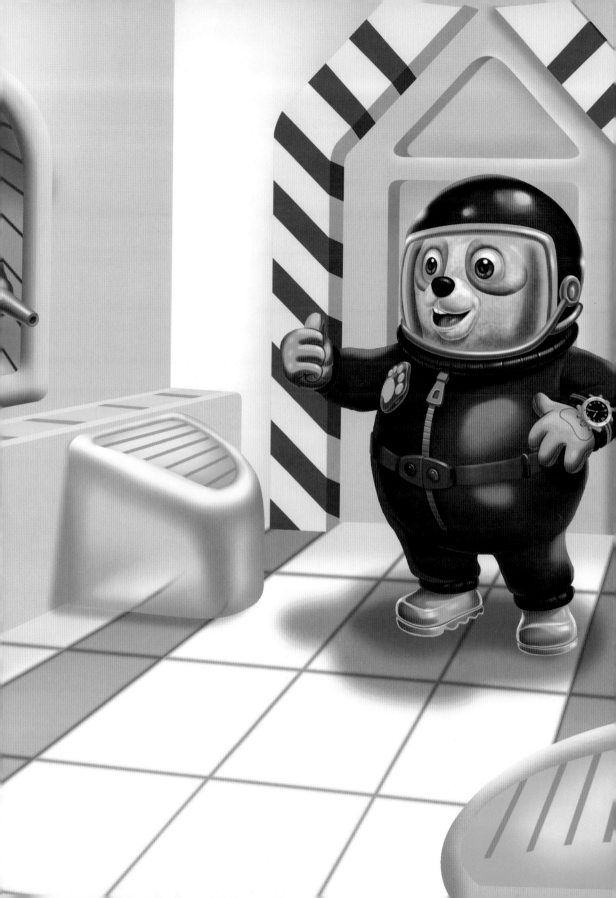

The paintball machines started firing.

"Oh, dear. What did Dottie tell me to do? First I look to the right?" Oso wondered aloud. "Hmmm, looks clear to me.

It must be safe to cross!"

Oso started walking. **SPLAT!** A yellow splash of paint landed on his left shoulder.

"Oops!" Oso blushed. "No worries – it's all part of the plan... more or less."

In the meantime, Shutter Bug had found someone in need of Agent Oso's help. It was Josie! Her neighbours were away, and she wasn't quite sure how to cross the street to get their post.

Paw Pilot began flashing her lights to let Oso know
that a special assignment was on its way:
SPECIAL ALERT! SPECIAL ALERT!

"Special Agent Oso? Mr Dos here. The postman just delivered some letters to Josie's neighbours' house and Josie needs your help! **Your special assignment: help her cross the road and retrieve their post.**"

Oso hopped into Whirlybird. "To Josie's house, Whirlybird – we have a special delivery to make! What's today's code name, Paw Pilot?"

Paw Pilot lit up. "When crossing the road, 'safety first' is my advice. Today's code name: **You Always Look Twice!**"

Josie was thrilled to see Special Agent Oso and Paw
Pilot. "So glad you're here! What should we do first?"

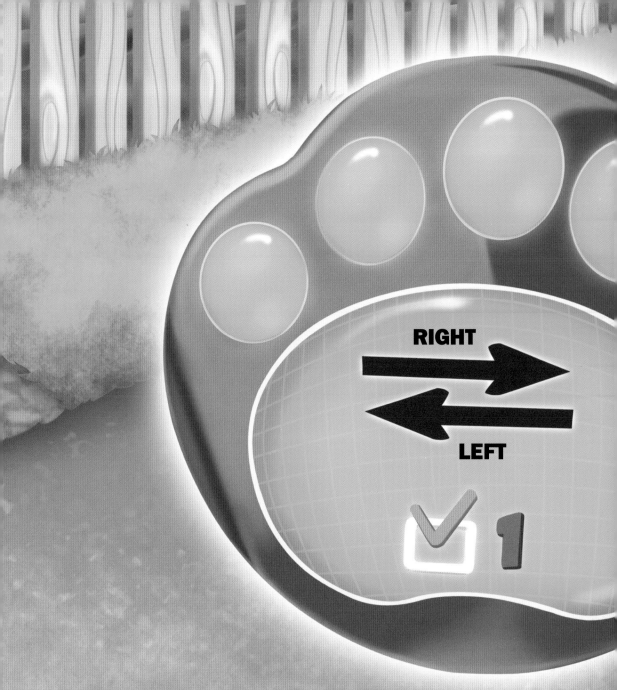

"Step one: look to the right and then to the left to make sure there's no traffic in either direction," said Paw Pilot.

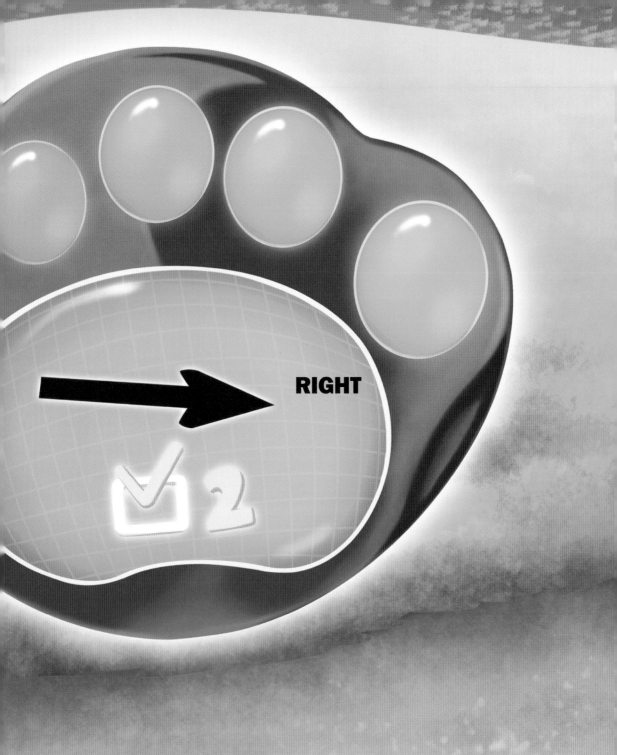

RIGHT

"Step two: now look to the right again, just to be sure the coast is clear," advised Paw Pilot.

"Aha!" cried Oso. "No wonder I got hit by the paintball. After I looked to my right, I forgot to look to my left and then look right again!"

"No traffic in either direction," Josie reported.

"Good! That means it's safe for us to cross the road and check your neighbours' postbox," said Oso. "Come on!"

"Great job, Josie – you did it!" Oso
cheered. "Now let's take the post home."

SAFE TO CROSS!

"Ready to cross the street again?" asked Paw Pilot.
"Just follow these three special steps."

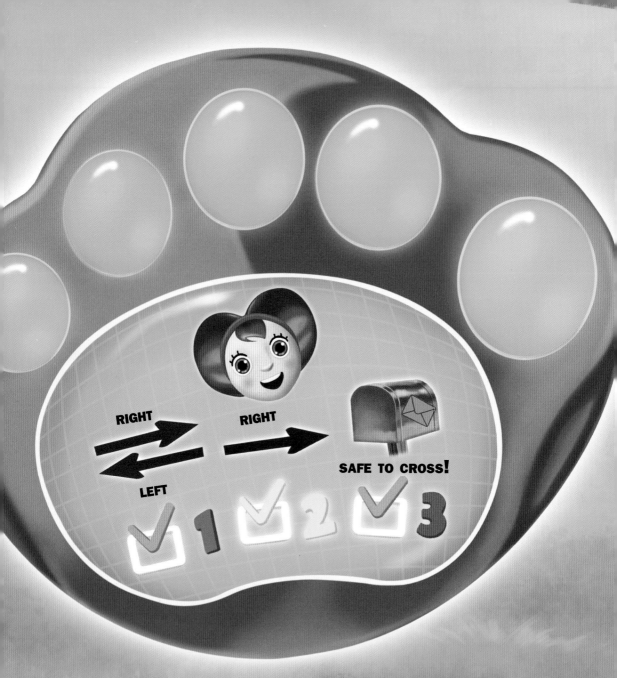

Josie and Oso need to use Paw Pilot's three special steps again to cross the road. Do you remember what they need to do for each step?

First, they need to look to the right and then to the left for traffic. **Next,** they need to look right again. **Finally,** if it's all clear, then it's safe to cross the road!

"Assignment complete!" shouted Oso.
"Thanks, Special Agent Oso." Josie smiled.
"I couldn't have done it without your help!"

MICKEY MOUSE CLUBHOUSE

Space Adventure

Based on the episode
written by Kevin D. Campbell,
Don Gillies & Mark Seidenberg

Welcome to Adventure Day at the Mickey Mouse Clubhouse! Mickey and the gang have a treasure map from Professor Von Drake. They're going to the Moon, to Mars, to Saturn – and to a mystery planet – to find a treasure!

Space Captain Mickey says, "Let's go, space adventurers!"

"Not so fast!" says the Professor. He explains that along the way, Mickey and the gang must find ten Treasure Stars. These stars will lead them to the mystery planet – and to the treasure!

Blast off!

Everyone is on board – even Toodles. They count down: ten, nine, eight, seven, six, five, four, three, two, one...

The gang doesn't know that someone is spying on them! It's Space Pirate Pete!

"Arrgh!" he says. "That space treasure will be mine!"

Pete has a new helper named Quoodles. He asks her for something to stop Mickey's ship. Quoodles brings a milk carton.

"What good is a milk carton?" asks Pete. "Oh, I get it. All those milk cartons will block the rocket!"

"Look at all that milk," says Goofy. "This must be the Milky Way!"

Space Pirate Pete says, "You're surrounded by milk.
Give up the treasure map!"
"No way!" says Mickey. "We need a Mouseketool.
Oh, Toodles!"

But Toodles doesn't show up. Where is he?

Toodles sees Quoodles outside the ship. Toodles has never seen anyone else who looks like him! They smile at each other and make silly faces.

"Oh, TOODLES!" calls Mickey.

Toodles hears Mickey. He smiles goodbye to Quoodles.

Toodles brings a Mouseketool. It's a giant cookie! The cookie floats away and the milk cartons follow it into space.

"Oh, space sticks!" says Space Pirate Pete. "Foiled again!"

Minnie giggles. "Everyone knows milk goes with cookies."

On the Moon, Mickey meets Moon-Man Chip and Moon-Man Dale. Mickey asks if they have seen any Treasure Stars.

"We see lots of space junk," they say. "We put it all in our Moon Locker."

"Then take us to your locker!" says Space Captain Mickey.

Moon-Men Chip and Dale lead them to their locker.
Goofy opens it.

"I think they need a bigger locker," says Goofy.

Hot dog! There are Treasure Stars one, two and three!

The Treasure Stars fly to the spaceship and stick on like magic!
"Now we're ready to go to our next stop," says Mickey.
"Mars, here we come!"

On Mars, Mickey meets Martian Mickey – and Pluto from Pluto! Mickey asks Martian Mickey if he knows where to find any Treasure Stars.

Martian Mickey says, "They may be in the Star Tree Forest!"

Meanwhile, back at the ship, Toodles sees Quoodles again. He gives her some flowers. But Pirate Pete stops by.

"Quoodles," he says, "stop your dillydallyin'. We gotta get that treasure map!" Quoodles has to go. Poor Toodles!

Martian Mickey takes the gang to the Star Tree Forest. "We don't have many trees on Mars, so every tree is a forest," he says.

Stars four, five and six are on the tree. They fly off and go straight to the rocket ship.

Space Pirate Pete has another trick up his sleeve.
He pretends to be a little old lady who is lost in space.
The little old lady asks Goofy for a map.
"Goofy, nooooo!" says Donald.
But it's too late. Goofy gives Pete the treasure map!

Goofy sure goofed. They've got to get the map back! Mickey, Goofy and Donald chase Pete around the rings of Saturn, but they can't catch that tricky space pirate. Then Mickey falls off the rings and floats away into outer space. Oh, no!

Mickey bumps into space rocks until Pluto rescues him.

"Thanks, Pluto," says Mickey.

Pluto and Mickey fly back to Saturn and the ship. On the way, they find the last Treasure Stars: seven, eight, nine and ten!

Back on Saturn, Toodles brings a Mouseketool - a big birdcage - to trap Pete. Donald grabs the map! But then Quoodles brings one of her tools. It's a Space Chicken to help Pete get away!

Now Mickey and his crew have the map and all ten Treasure Stars. The stars light the way to the mystery planet.

"Hey, that planet looks familiar," says Goofy. "Let's call it Planet Mickey!"

The stars shine on the *X* that marks the spot.

And it's off to Planet Mickey to find the treasure!

Uh-oh. Space Pirate Pete gets to Planet Mickey first and finds the *X* that marks the treasure spot. Pete has one last trick. He throws out a sticky web.

"Now when those little space adventurers try to pass through here and get the treasure, they'll get stuck!" says Pete.

But it's Quoodles who gets stuck in the web.
"Poor Quoodles," says Pete. "I gotta rescue you!"
"Help!" yells Pete. "Somebody HELP!"
Mickey hears him and comes right away.

But now Toodles gets stuck in the sticky web, too!
"What can we do?" asks Pete.

Mickey says, "I'm going to use a Mouseketool!"
"That's a great idea," says Pete. "And I'll use a
Quoodles tool!"

Even though he is stuck, Toodles sends Mickey a Mouseketool. It is... Space Pirate Pete! And Quoodles' tool is... Mickey the Space Captain Mouse! "What can it mean?" asks Pete.

"It means we can save Toodles and Quoodles if we work together as friends!" says Mickey.

Mickey and Pete jump up and down on the arch holding the web. The arch breaks. Toodles and Quoodles are free!

Everyone is happy to meet Quoodles – and to see that Pete has given up his 'piratey' ways. Pluto points to the X. He knows where to dig. Pluto digs up the treasure chest. Inside is Professor Von Drake's remote control.

Minnie says, "Push the button, Mickey!"

The ground shakes and up comes...

...the Mickey Mouse Space House! What a terrific treasure!

Martian Mickey says, "Now when you visit us, you'll have a fun place to play."

"Hot dog!" says Mickey.

Everyone does the out-of-this-world Hot-Dog Dance!

As Mickey and the gang head back to their
Clubhouse on Earth, Martian Mickey waves.
"Thanks for stopping by!"

MICKEY MOUSE CLUBHOUSE

Goofy Goes to the Doctor

By Susan Amerikaner
Illustrated by Loter, Inc.

Mickey woke up early and checked the date. Yep. Today Goofy was supposed to go to the doctor for a check-up. This afternoon, Mickey would drive Goofy to his appointment.

Ding-dong!

Who was ringing the Mousekedoorbell?

It was Goofy the Great!
Mickey yawned and said, "Goof, you're early!"
"Early for what?" replied Goofy.
"Aw," said Mickey. "Did you forget that your
check-up with the doctor is this afternoon?

"Garwsh. I *did* forget," said Goofy. "I came to show you some new magic tricks. But now that you reminded me about the doctor, I'm gonna show you one of my greatest tricks ever. Hokeypokey!"

Goofy the Great disappeared! That was
a good trick.
Mickey called, "Goof, where are you?"

Pluto pointed to a clue.

"The Silly Switch!" said Mickey. "Good job, Pluto!"

Goofy had pulled the Silly Switch to disappear.

"Let's pull it again and see where he went," said Mickey.

They found Goofy. He was at the Moo Mart – inside a barrel of apples!

"What are you doing in there, Goof?" asked Mickey.

"An apple a day keeps the doctor away," said Goofy.

"So if I eat this whole barrel, I'll *never* have to go to the doctor!"

"That's *udderly* ridiculous," said Clarabelle.

Goofy and Mickey went back to the Clubhouse. Daisy came to visit, and Mickey told her why Goofy looked so glum.

"Hmmm," said Daisy. "This would be a good time for me to play Dr Daisy, but I don't have my pretend-doctor bag."

"We can fix that," said Mickey. He called, "Oh, Toodles!"

"Thanks, Toodles," said Daisy.

"The doctor will examine parts of your body, such as your ears," said Dr Daisy.

"That's an *otoscope*," said Mickey.

"Very good, pretend-patient Mickey!" said Dr Daisy.

Goofy asked, "Does that hurt?"

"Nope. Not a bit," said Mickey.

"Garwsh," said Goofy. "You've got the biggest ears in town, so if it doesn't hurt you, it won't hurt me!"

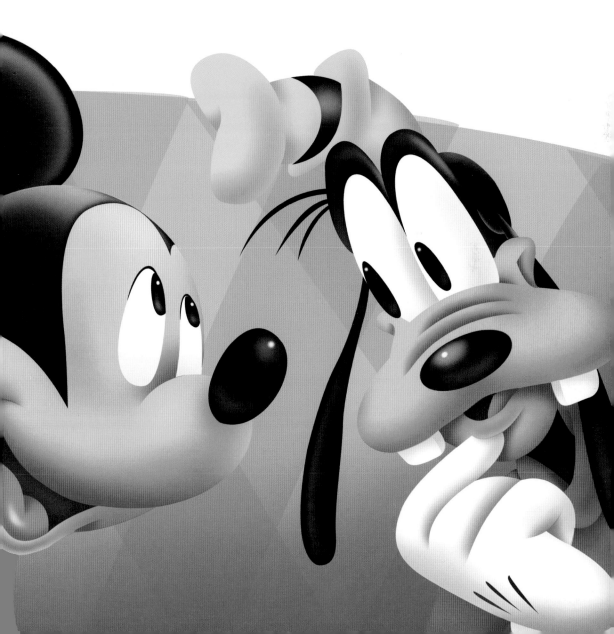

Next, Daisy said that the doctor uses a *stethoscope* to listen to heartbeats.

Goofy said, "Hy-yuck! Then I guess it's a good thing I wore these today!"

"Oh, Goof." Mickey laughed. "Not *those* hearts. Your *real* heart – the one inside your body!"

Daisy listened to Mickey's heart.
"What does it sound like?" asked Goofy.
Daisy said, "It goes *lub-dub, lub-dub*. Here,
Goofy," Daisy continued, "you try it."
"What do you hear?" asked Mickey.
"Fi-fi-fo-fum!" said Goofy.
"Huh?" said Mickey
"Hi, there!" called Willie the Giant.

Willie the friendly giant wanted to help, too.

"When I go to the doctor," said Willie, "my favourite part is getting to stick out my tongue and say AHH. Then the doctor can examine my throat."

Willie showed them how he does it. "AHHHH," he roared.

"Oh, boy," said Mickey. "Thanks, Willie. We get the idea!"

Goofy was starting to feel better. "So that's it?" he asked.

"That's most of it," said Daisy. "Um, you might also need to get an... injection."

"Oh, no!" hollered Goofy. "Don't come near me with that pointy thing! Besides, I'm not sick!"

Daisy explained that sometimes the doctor gives you an injection with medicine to stop you from getting sick.

"But it's *gotta* hurt," said Goofy.

"Not as much as you think," said Daisy.

"That reminds me," said Mickey, "I have a thinking trick that I use when I get an injection."

"Do you make the doctor disappear?" asked Goofy.

"Nope," said Mickey. "I close my eyes and think about things that I like, then I count them. Can you guess what I think about?"

"Hot dogs!" said Goofy.

"You betcha," said Mickey. "By the time I count three of them, it's all over."

"Say, that *is* a neat trick," said Goofy. "I think I'll count ice cream sundaes!"

It was time for Goofy and Mickey to go. Daisy reminded them that they might have to sit in the doctor's waiting room for a little while. "So it's a good idea to bring a book or a toy you like," said Daisy.

"Another good idea. Be right back," said Goofy. "I'll meet you by the car."

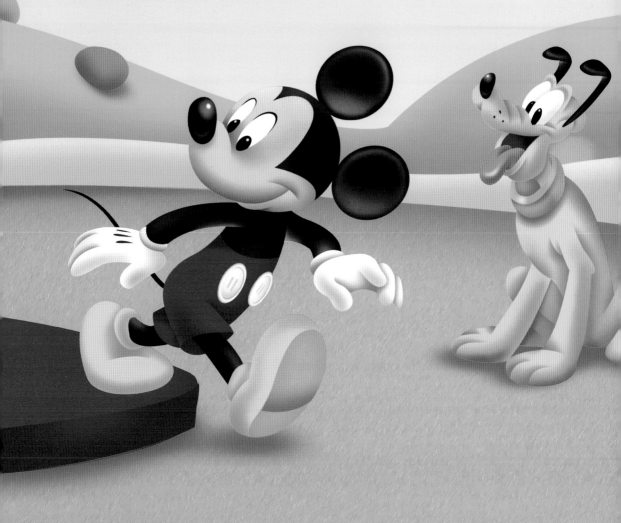

"We won't have to wait *that* long, Goof," said Mickey. "And we can't fit all that into the car!"

Goofy thought for a few minutes. Then he said, "If I can't bring all my stuff, can I bring all my friends instead?"

"Great idea, Goofy," said Mickey, smiling.

Finally, Goofy did go to the doctor – and he brought along the whole gang. Hot diggety dog!

MICKEY MOUSE CLUBHOUSE

Look Before You Leap

By Sheila Sweeny Higginson
Illustrated by the Disney Storybook Artists
Designed by Elizabeth Andaluz

Mickey and Goofy were enjoying a quiet game of chess. Just as Mickey was about to make a move, something soared through the window and landed right in the middle of the chessboard.

"What was that?" Mickey asked. The two friends looked carefully at something that looked right back at them.

It was green. It had webbed feet. It said, "Ribbit, ribbit."

It was a frog – a very jumpy frog. Goofy tried to grab it. PLOP! The frog leaped out of Goofy's hands and right onto the silly switch. The room began to spin around. Mickey tried to grab the frog, but it leaped right towards the...

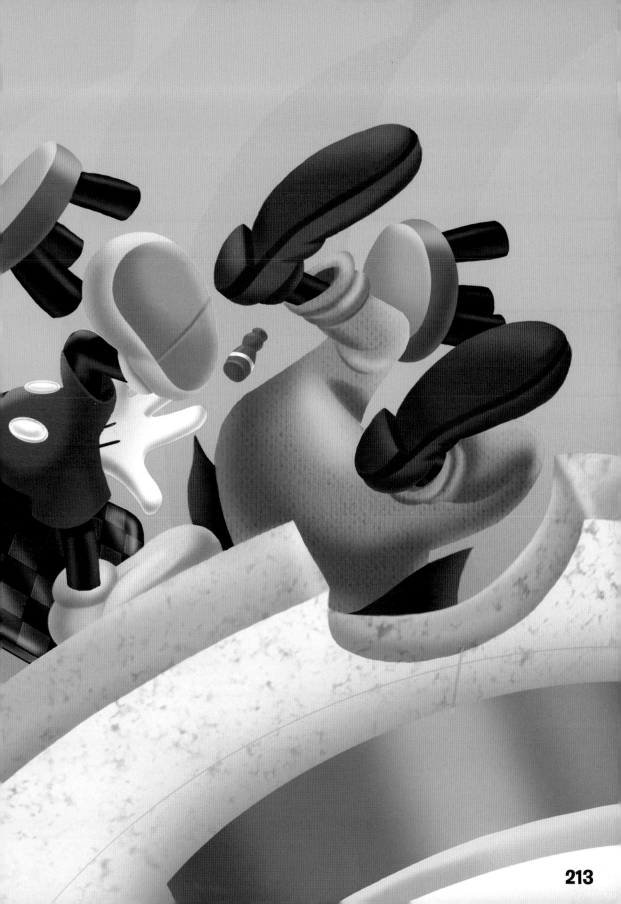

...kitchen sink. KERPLUNK!

"You really should look before you leap!" Mickey said to the frog.

"What are we going to do about this big puddle?" Goofy asked.

"Oh, Toodles!" Mickey called. "We need some Mouseketools - right now!"

"The mop is the right tool for this job," said Mickey. "Thanks, Toodles!" All of Mickey's hard work made Goofy hungry. He decided to make lunch. Just then, the frog took a giant leap right towards...

...Goofy's sandwich. SQUISH!

"Stop!" Mickey cried as Goofy was about to take a bite.

"You really should look before you leap," Goofy said to the frog, "and I should look before I bite!"

Goofy carried the frog outside.

"Hold on tight," Mickey said. "He's pretty slippery."

"I have him.... I have him.... OOPS! I don't have him!"

Goofy yelped as the frog leaped right towards...

...Daisy's painting! SPLAT!

"You should look before you leap!" Daisy said as the paint splattered all around. "Now my painting – and my clothes – are a mess."

"Hey there, little friend," Mickey said to the frog. "Slow down!"
But it was too late. The frog leaped out from behind Daisy's painting and headed straight towards...

...Mickey's bicycle. BOING! He zoomed down the road, holding tightly to the handlebars. He was headed straight for a cliff.

"Oh, no!" Goofy shouted.

"Oh, Toodles!" yelled Mickey. "We need you!"

"The lasso is the right tool for this job," said Mickey. "Thanks, Toodles!"

Mickey and Goofy carefully pulled the bicycle back from the edge of the cliff.

"I think we should help our friend the frog find a nice, safe pond," Mickey said. "Then he can leap without causing any trouble."

The frog jumped up and down in
agreement.
　　Then he hopped away down the road with
Mickey and Goofy following fast behind him.

The frog stopped hopping right in front
of the pizzeria.
Slowly, Mickey and Goofy crept up behind him.
"We've got to get him before he leaps!" Mickey
whispered. But it was too late. Just as Mickey
reached for him, the frog leaped right onto a...

...pizza pie. SLOSH!

"You should look before you leap!" shouted the man behind the counter as tomato sauce dripped off the pizza. The frog stopped for a moment to lick himself off.

Then he hopped down Main Street, headed right towards Minnie and Pluto.

"Maybe Minnie and Pluto can help us catch our frog friend and bring him to a nice pond," Mickey shouted.

But the frog had other ideas. He took a great big leap and landed right inside...

...the goldfish bowl. SPLASH!

The big wave made the goldfish fly right out. Minnie gently put the goldfish back into its bowl. "I don't know if we'll ever find a pond for froggie. We need some help!" Goofy sighed.

"Oh, Toodles!" Mickey called.

"The net is the right tool for this job," said Mickey.
At last, they held the frog safely in the net.

"He seems sad," Goofy said.

"I think you're right, Goofy," Mickey agreed.
Then he looked up ahead and saw something
that made him – and the frog – smile.

"I think we've found just the right place
for you, froggie," Mickey said.

The friends walked quickly down the street towards the fountain. Carefully, Mickey placed the net on the ground and began to lift the frog out. But the frog couldn't wait. Out he hopped, headed straight for the...

...fountain. He landed with a
SPLOSH! right next to another frog.
"Ribbit, ribbit," he said.
"Ribbit, ribbit," she replied.

"Maybe we didn't find a pond," said Mickey, "but we did
   find a good place for him to splash and leap."
   "We've found the frog a friend, too," noticed Minnie.
"And they look very happy to see each other!"
   "I think Minnie's goldfish is happy, too!" added Goofy.

Later, while Donald, Minnie and Daisy made dinner,
Mickey and Goofy got back to their game of chess.

"C'mon, Mickey," Goofy said, "you haven't made a move in a long time."

"I know, I know," replied Mickey. "I just want to make sure I look carefully before I leap!"

I finished
this book on

....